NOVEL NEWS

Using the Newspaper to Analyze Literature

Teacher Guide

Written by
Ellen Doukoullos

ISBN 1-58130-596-6

To order, contact your local school
supply store, or—

Novel Units, Inc.
P.O. Box 791610
San Antonio, TX 78279

Web site: www.educyberstor.com

Table of Contents

Introduction

Skills Taught in This Program
- analyzing
- organizing
- editing
- revising
- vocabulary selection
- comparing and contrasting
- synthesizing
- researching
- writing a topic sentence
- using appropriate detail
- summarizing
- drawing conclusions
- sequencing
- observing
- scanning

Students Will Learn to
- write concisely
- use powerful vocabulary
- use facts from fiction accurately
- read for detail
- work in a team

Students Can Work on These Lessons
- independently in class or as homework
- in pairs
- in collaborative groups (with assigned individual tasks/roles)

Writing Forms Included in the Lessons
- essay
- ad (classified and display)
- caption for photograph
- headline
- news story (inverted pyramid and chronological format)
- comic strip
- descriptive article

Tools for each Lesson
- newspapers
- copies of Student Activity Sheet
- lesson plan
- dictionaries
- thesauri
- scissors (optional)
- marking pens (optional)

How to Use These Lessons
First, choose a novel. (Note: While these lessons focus on the novel form, they can be adapted to short stories, plays, and even a long poem.)

Second, read through the lesson plans and review the activity sheets. Schedule the assignments to coincide with the pacing of the novel. Students will need to have read enough about the character in order to complete some of the lessons.

Third, assemble your tools.

Culminating Class Project
Each lesson connects the novel with a different part of the newspaper. Therefore, be sure to save the best examples of student work *from each lesson* for the final project of creating an entire newspaper based on the novel. If you feel an entire newspaper is too big a project, cut it down to creating a front page and a "lifestyle" section, which could also include comics.

Correlation to the English-Language Arts Framework

Many states are developing, or have already developed, goals and objectives for their English-language arts curriculum. *Novel News* was prepared with California goals in mind, but is helpful to English teachers in all states.

> "In summary, the English-language arts curriculum must provide students, through their study and understanding of literature and their experiences in listening, speaking, reading, and writing, with a level of literacy and fluency that enables them to become informed and responsible citizens, competent and successful members of the work force, and thinking, fulfilled individuals within our society." (California Framework, page 4)

Using the newspaper fulfills the three "overarching" goals of the English-language arts curriculum:

- *To prepare all students to function as informed and effective citizens in our democratic society.*
  The newspaper reports "bad" news because it is the job of citizens to take action to turn bad news into "good" news. Information is the beginning. When students study the newspaper, they learn how to analyze facts for their significance and how to communicate their opinions about what should be done to solve reported problems.

- *To prepare all students to function effectively in the world of work.*
  The newspaper directly connects students to the workplace. Students read about changes in the economy, jobs, and local businesses on the business pages. When they write about their future aspirations, their writing is based on reality. Using the newspaper to improve listening and speaking skills gives students lifelong skills.

- *To prepare all students to realize personal fulfillment.*
  The newspaper is real human drama, the stuff of fiction. Students read about the successes and failures of others. Through comparing real people with fictional characters, students develop goals and attitudes which develop their individual talents. (California Framework, pages 1–2)

> "Instructional programs that emphasize the integration of listening, speaking, reading, and writing and the teaching of language skills in meaningful contexts…" (California Framework, page 3)

Novel News features lessons that integrate listening, speaking, reading, and writing with the teaching of language skills, as prescribed by the California Framework.

The Newspaper Habit...

Research for more than 20 years has confirmed this important fact about reading—students who get "the newspaper habit" score significantly higher on reading comprehension, vocabulary, and writing tests.

Beyond tests, this good habit keeps students reading. It connects them with their community as young adults and throughout their lives.

"Print media, such as newspapers...offer resources to lure even reluctant readers to become involved with language and learning. This is true whether the task is reading a driver's manual or cookbook, a career file or job application, a classic or a vision of the future. For example, by reading *The Wind in the Willows, The Velveteen Rabbit, The Little Prince, The Prince and the Pauper, The Secret Garden*, and *The Invisible Man*, students can discover the magic of language that transports them beyond today into the past and future, beyond their homes and schools to anywhere in the world or the solar system, and beyond the ordinary to the extraordinary world of imaginative human experience in good literature. In a world full of language experiences and opportunities, students must inevitably discover the limitless possibilities of learning as they explore the world of books and print and other language media."

(California Framework, pages 8–9)

"Daily experiences...enable students to become fluent and confident about writing while they also learn to write for real audiences and meaningful purposes by, for example, communicating with other classes or school officials or writing letters to local newspapers or politicians."

"Finally, students must develop a sense that something happens after writing—that writing is published or posted for reading and that writing can be mailed or illustrated. Students must also learn that the act of meaningful writing goes beyond the assigning of a letter grade by a teacher..."

"Informal discussions help students learn to listen attentively to what others are saying, to evaluate and respond, and to incorporate what they hear into their own thinking and responding. Discussions between partners or in small groups help students learn to state opinions honestly, precisely, and tactfully to discover multiple viewpoints on a difficult issue and to negotiate and find common ground..."

"...students who have been involved in their own learning through listening, speaking, reading, and writing will enter a society prepared for the kind of cooperative work needed in the adult world today, a world where intellectual negotiation is essential to corporate, social, and political problem-solving. Their experiences in role-playing, leadership, and decision-making—for example, when they plan classroom publications cooperatively, dramatize reactions to a novel, or engage in formal speaking situations—provide models for comparable roles in their lives."

(California Framework, pages 10–12)

Classroom Assessment

"Teachers, students, and parents are offered a more accurate picture of students' facility with English-language arts by using a variety of assessment strategies, such as the following:

• Classroom discussion of a literary work on a classwide or small-group basis provides much information about students' understanding of a work.

• Carefully planned teacher-designed questions, to focus students' learning, or opportunities for students to learn to phrase questions for each other require students to go beyond yes or no answers to the use of higher-order thinking processes.

• Assuming the role of a literary character who writes a letter to another character, an editor, or a governmental leader reflects the students' insights into the character's values and motives.

• Rewriting a piece in a different genre...reflects understanding of meaning, tone, voice, and character.

• Students' extensive reading of books, magazines, and newspapers in leisure time indicates that reading is an activity of choice and pleasure."

(California Framework, pages 34–35 [partial list])

Writing...Personal Ads for Fictional Characters

Outcome
Students will write concisely and select powerful words.

Skills Used
Editing, revising, scanning, character analysis.

Preparation
Choose a selection rich in detail about a character in the work your students are reading. Locate the personal ads in the newspaper (often on Friday) and select one to use as a model. Reproduce Activity Sheet #1. Have newspapers available.

Ask
What words best describe you? Make a list of the words you think describe you. You will not share these words with anyone. Discuss how different words describe body type and others describe personality or interests.

Objective
Tell students today they will learn how to write a personal ad for a character in a novel.

Model
Have students find one sentence in the novel that describes something about a character's looks and one paragraph that describes a character's interests or personality. Discuss by making two lists on board. Indicate page numbers for future reference (checking for accuracy).

Activity Sheet
Distribute. *Assign Steps 1 and 2.* Circulate around the room to see if students are choosing unmarried characters over the age of 18 and if they are finding physical descriptions and interests.

Newspapers
Distribute. Go through a model ad for Step 3. Count the words in this model ad. *Assign Steps 3 and 4.*

Circulate around the room and guide students in writing concise, accurate ads that describe their characters and explain what kind of person the character would logically want to meet—consistent with the storyline. After students write their first draft, have them count the words. Limit: 30 words. Revise to fit.

Followup Discussion
Read finished ads aloud. Discuss accuracy for the character and the plot. Save for newspaper project at end of this unit.

Ask
What questions does the advertising rep need to ask the caller? (What are your interests, hobbies? How would you describe yourself? What are you seeking in a mate?)

Background on Newspaper Careers in Advertising
Newspapers employ people who help individuals write their ads over the phone. Students who enjoy this exercise should be encouraged to watch the employment ads for telephone sales positions in the Classified Advertising department of the newspaper. This is an entry-level position.

Skills needed: good command of the English language and excellent spelling skills; good speaking and listening skills; type (keyboard) 45 wpm; outgoing, friendly personality; work well under pressure; excellent customer service attitude; high school education or better; one year sales background helpful; complete all paperwork accurately, neatly.

Classified ads are the largest source of income for all newspapers. Display ads are the second-greatest source of income. Subscriptions and newsrack sales are third in income.

Writing…a Personal Ad for a Fictional Character

Title of Novel: _____

Name of Character in Novel: _____
(Note: character must be unmarried and over 18.)

Pretend you are this character. You are single and want to find a special person.

1. Search through the novel and make a list of this character's looks. Note page numbers
    (   ) where you find information:

    _____

    _____

    _____

2. Search through the novel and make a list of this character's interests. Ask yourself: What
    activities does this character like? Note page numbers where you find information:

    _____

    _____

    _____

    _____

    _____

    _____

3. Find the personal ads in this newspaper. Underline words that describe how the person
    looks. Then circle words that tell the person's interests.

4. Now, use a piece of scratch paper to practice writing your character's personal ad. **You
    have 30 words for your ad.** Your ad should include: how the character looks, what the
    character likes to do, and what kind of person the character wants to meet **based on facts
    in the book.** Revise your ad. Use the most appealing words to attract the right person for
    your character. Then, write your finished ad below.

    _____

    _____

    _____

    _____

    _____

    _____

    _____

    _____

    _____

Writing...about Emotions of Fictional Characters and Real People

Outcome
Students will be able to write an analytical essay comparing the emotions of characters with the emotions of real people in the news.

Skills Used
Research, analysis, compare and contrast, synthesis.

Preparation
Scan today's newspaper and note stories and photos containing much emotion. Review the emotions of characters in the novel. Select a passage about an emotion of one character. Select an item from the newspaper showing this emotion to use as a model. Reproduce Activity Sheet #2. Have newspapers available.

Motivation
Ask students to make a list of emotions. Share orally. Categorize into "positive" and "negative" emotions.

Ask
Which emotions are for real people and which are for fictional characters? (all for both)

Objective
Tell students today they will research and confirm that emotions found in fiction are found in real life. Then they will write about what they have discovered.

Model
Discuss the character's emotion and the news item you've prepared. Read the news item aloud.

Activity Sheet
Distribute. Form pairs. *Assign Step 1.* Circulate around the room and check to see if students are finding emotions and situations in the plot.

Newspapers
Distribute. *Assign Step 2.* Circulate.

Discussion
In preparation for Step 3 (writing the essay) discuss the research as a class. Ask students to think about situations in their own lives where the same emotions found in the newspaper and in the novel have been expressed. *Assign Step 3*, the essay, of appropriate length for your students. Review the parts of an essay. Establish due date for first draft. Establish revision dates.

Background on Newswriting
News accounts initially give the basic facts of an emotional story, often a tragedy. A follow-up, in-depth, feature story will go into the feelings of the participants. The reporter will interview the survivors or participants at length and write an "aftermath" type story, often called a "human interest" story.

Columnists sometimes use these kinds of stories as a basis for writing an essay-style column, sometimes in a philosophical tone.

Writing...about Emotions of Fictional Characters and Real People

Title of Novel: _____

Name of Character in Novel: _____

1. Find two examples of emotions this character has shown in this novel.

   EMOTION #1 _____

      WHEN? _____ (page) _____

      WHY? _____ (page) _____

   EMOTION #2: _____

      WHEN? _____ (page) _____

      WHY? _____ (page) _____

2. In the newspaper, find an article or a photograph that shows a real-life person experiencing these same emotions. Clip and explain below.

   Headline: _____

   Emotion: _____

   Why? _____

   Headline: _____

   Emotion: _____

   Why? _____

3. On another sheet of paper, write an essay giving your opinion about emotions in fiction and in real life. Include examples from this research you have just completed.

Writing...a Lost-and-Found Ad for a Fictional Animal

Outcome
Students will be able to describe an animal's physical attributes and identify the emotions a character feels for an animal in the story.

Skills Used
Research, analysis, synthesis, vocabulary selection.

Preparation
Choose a selection rich in detail about an animal in the novel your students are reading. Also choose a selection that describes a human character's feelings for the animal. Locate the lost-and-found ads in the Classified section of your local newspaper. Reproduce Activity Sheet #3. Have newspapers available.

Ask
What does your pet look like? What does your pet mean to you?

Objective
Tell the students today they will learn how to write a lost-and-found ad based on an animal in the novel they are reading.

Model
Using the selections you have chosen, discuss the difference between the words that describe the physical characteristics and the words that describe emotional needs. Physical facts versus the subtleties of emotions require different thinking and writing skills. Explore both with students first.

Activity Sheet
Distribute. *Assign steps 1–2.* Circulate around the room to see if students understand the difference between physical facts and subtle emotions.

Newspapers
Distribute. *Assign steps 3–5.* After students write the first draft, have them count the words. *Assign Steps 6–7.* Limit: 20 words. Revise to fit.

Followup Discussion
Read finished ads aloud. Discuss accuracy about the animal and the human character in the story. Save for newspaper project at the end of this unit.

Independent Practice
Students role-play: one student is the human character calling the newspaper for help in writing his or her ad. The other student is the advertising rep, helping the caller write the ad.

Ask
What questions does the advertising rep need to ask the caller? What does your dog look like? What does your dog mean to you? Are you offering a reward? What is your phone number?

Homework to Involve Parents
Interview your parents about a pet they have lost. Write a lost-and-found ad for the pet.

Background on Newspaper Careers in Advertising
See Teacher Plan #1.

Writing...a Lost-and-Found Ad for a Fictional Animal

Title of Novel: _____

Animal's Name: _____

Type of Animal: _____

(Note: give the page number where you find information, for future reference.)

1. Describe the animal's looks: _____
   _____
   _____
   _____
   _____

2. Tell what the animal means to its owner: _____
   _____
   _____
   _____
   _____

3. Find the lost-and-found ads for animals in the Classified section of the newspaper. Choose one ad. Underline words that describe the animal.

4. Circle the words that describe what the animal means to the person who lost it.

5. Now, on a piece of scratch paper, draft a lost-and-found ad for the animal in the novel. You have 20 words to describe the animal and tell why its owner wants it back. Remember, be true to the story.

6. Revise your ad so it uses powerful words to encourage someone to find and return the animal. Limit: 20 words.

7. Write the final ad: _____
   _____
   _____
   _____
   _____
   _____

Writing...a Help-Wanted Ad for a Fictional Character

Outcome
Students will be able to identify a character's status and skills in the context of the novel.

Skills Used
Research, analysis, application of information.

Preparation
Choose a selection rich in detail about the place where a character works in the novel your students are reading. Locate the employment ("Help-Wanted") ads in the Classified section of your local newspaper. Scan for jobs that might apply to the character. Note if none are available. Reproduce Activity Sheet #4. Have newspapers available.

Ask
What kind of jobs do you do at home or in the workplace? What skills do you need for these jobs? How did you get your jobs? What must you do to keep your jobs?

Objective
Tell the students today they will learn how to write a Help-Wanted ad for the occupation of a character in a novel.

Activity Sheet
Distribute. *Assign Steps 1–2.* Guide to appropriate pages. Circulate and help students identify the character's skills. Discuss.

Newspapers
Distribute. Guide students in finding the employment ads. Use the index to locate Classified section. *Assign Step 3.* Circulate and help students with vocabulary. Discuss. *Assign Step 4.* After students write first draft, have them count the words. Revise to fit space for 40 words. Read words aloud. Discuss accuracy for the character in the work students are reading. Discuss words that seem to make the job appealing. Save the best ads for the class newspaper project.

Independent Practice
Assign an essay in which students will discuss the character's degree of success on the job in the novel and explain why the character will or will not be successful.

Extra Activity
Submit the best ads to the school newspaper as a humorous quiz for all students.

Extra Credit
Assign students to read the Business page in the newspaper, then write an article announcing a character's business success or failure.

Background on Newspaper Careers in Advertising
Telephone salespeople in the Classified Advertising Department receive calls from employment agencies and Human Resource (Personnel) Directors at corporations. The salespeople assist the callers in choosing the right category for the ad, writing the headline and the copy (words) for the ad. This position requires accurate spelling and vocabulary skills, and listening and writing skills.

Writing...a Help-Wanted Ad for a Fictional Character

Title of Novel: _____

Name of Character: _____

Character's Occupation: _____

1. Research the novel and list what skills this occupation requires in the novel.

   _____
   _____
   _____
   _____
   _____
   _____
   _____
   _____

2. Describe the place where the character works: _____

   _____
   _____
   _____
   _____
   _____

3. Look at the Help-Wanted ads in the Classified section of the newspaper. Circle the ads your character is qualified for.

4. Suppose this character is looking for this job before the novel begins. Write an employment ad this character would answer, based on the skills needed. You have 40 words plus a headline for the ad. Use scratch paper to compose, then revise. Use words that would attract your character to the job, but be accurate about the type of setting. After revising, write your finished ad below.

   _____
   _____
   _____
   _____
   _____
   _____
   _____
   _____
   _____
   _____

Writing...an Editorial about a Problem in a Novel

Outcome
Students will be able to identify a fictional problem and develop their opinions about it in an editorial (essay).

Skills Used
Analysis, writing a topic sentence, using appropriate detail, summarizing, drawing conclusions.

Preparation
Review the editorials in today's local newspaper. Review news, ads, columns, comics for problems. Choose a selection from a work your students are currently reading that describes a character's problem. Reproduce Activity Sheet #5. Have newspapers available.

Newspapers
Distribute. Have students identify problems reported anywhere in the newspaper: in the news reports, the comics, advice columns—even advertising. List problems on the chalkboard.

Objective
Tell students today they will identify a problem in the novel they are reading. Then they will write an Editorial (essay) giving their opinion with solutions to the problem.

Model
Have students turn to the Opinion page in the newspaper. Opinions appear in three forms: the Editorial (unsigned, at left), Letters to the Editor (signed), and opinion columns on both the Editorial page and Op-Ed page (**Op**posite the **Ed**itorial page) (signed). Have students identify the problem in one editorial.

Ask
What is the editorial writer's solution to the problem?

Activity Sheet
Distribute Student Activity Sheet. *Assign Step 1* (another editorial or column or letter to editor). Discuss. *Assign Step 2*. Discuss the different problems faced by different fictional characters. List on the board.

Independent Practice
Assign Step 3 (the essay/editorial). Students write first draft of Editorial. Students later discuss round-robin in collaborative groups. Rewrite. Assign due dates throughout. Save the best editorials for use with the class newspaper project at end of this unit.

Extra Activity
After students complete their editorials, have them exchange and write "letters to the editor" in response. They need to be "in character" to do so. Save for class newspaper project.

Homework to Involve Parents
Ask students to interview their parents about a problem in the news. Students gather opinions from parents, then write an editorial essay giving solutions.

Name: _____

Writing...an Editorial about a Problem in a Novel

Step 1: Read an editorial on the opinion page of the newspaper. Identify the problem and the opinion of the editor about solving the problem.

Headline (title) of Editorial: _____

Problem discussed in Editorial: _____

_____

Opinion of the editor (writer) of the Editorial about how to solve the problem:

_____

_____

_____

Step 2: Make an outline before you write. In the novel you are reading, identify a problem one of the character's is facing.

Character: _____

Character's problem: _____

_____

Step 3: Begin your first draft of the Editorial.

(a) State your opinion of the character's problem: _____

_____

_____

_____

_____

(b) Assume this problem exists in real life for many people. What are your solutions to the problem? List on the back of this sheet.

(c) The last paragraph of your Editorial will compare the fictional problem and real life. You should summarize your solutions forcefully. Start writing.

Writing...Headlines about Conflict

Outcome
Students will write concisely to fit within columns on a newspaper page.

Skills Used
Revising, choosing precise vocabulary, analysis.

Preparation
Review headlines on front page of today's local newspaper. Reproduce Activity Sheet #6. Have newspapers available.

Model
Hold up front page of newspaper.

Ask
What is a headline? What is the purpose of a headline? Where is the largest headline on this page? How does the headline writer know how many words to use?*

* The "count" for the headline is determined by the point size (height) of the typeface and the number of spaces in the line the typeface will fit. For today's lesson, students will simply count the characters and spaces rather than consider the point size or type face. Or, if a computer is available, the count can be demonstrated with various typefaces and point sizes within set margins.

Objective
Tell students today they will learn how to write a headline describing the conflict in one chapter of the novel they are currently reading.

Ask
In this chapter, who is in conflict with whom (or what, if a conflict with nature, for example). Write on board. What happens during the conflict? When does the conflict take place? Where does the conflict take place? Why is there a conflict?

Newspapers
Distribute. Ask students to read headlines and tell what the conflict is in each headline. Write on board. Compare newspaper conflicts with the conflict in this chapter. On the board, compose a headline for the conflict in the chapter you are working with. Make it fit within the same number of spaces as the largest headline on the front page. Example: if the headline is two lines of 20 spaces each, your chapter headline must fit that length.

Activity Sheet
Distribute and assign different chapters to different groups or pairs or individual students. Circulate and discuss the conflict in the various chapter conflicts with students. Review the length of the headline as students begin to do Step 2.

Discussion
Students share the work on their Activity Sheets. Save for class newspaper project at end of unit.

Name: _____

Writing...Headlines about Conflict

Title of Novel: _____

Chapter: _____ **Title of Chapter:** _____

1. Describe the main conflict in this chapter:_____

   Who is in conflict? _____

   What happens during the conflict? _____
   _____
   _____

   When does the conflict take place? _____

   Where does the conflict take place? _____

   Why is there a conflict? _____
   _____
   _____

2. If you have a computer available, select margins, select a typeface, select a point size, then go to Step 3. If you do not have a computer available, continue with these instructions: Using the newspaper, count the characters and spaces on each line of the largest headline on the front page of the main section.
   # of lines in the headline: _____
   # of characters and spaces in each line: _____

3. Go back to #1 and review the elements of the conflict in the chapter. Start writing your headline on scratch paper. Use an action verb. Choose words that describe the conflict fully. Read many headlines to give you ideas about your headline. Revise until you fit into the space allowed by your count in #2.

   Write your finished headline below. Use only the number of lines and the number of characters and spaces you listed in #2 above.

   _____
   _____
   _____
   _____
   _____
   _____
   _____
   _____

Writing...a News Story about Conflict

Outcome
Students will be able to write a news story from the facts they find in the novel they are reading.

Skills Used
Research, analysis, organization.

Preparation
Review today's newspaper's front page. Read through the first paragraph (lead—pronounced "leed") of several stories and identify WHO, WHAT, WHEN, WHERE, WHY facts. Sometimes HOW will be a key fact, too. The lead should be less than 20 words and use short sentences with succinct, even snappy vocabulary. The *very first words* must be the most important words in the lead. Lower paragraphs give information and background facts, in descending order of importance. This form of newswriting is called the Inverted Pyramid.

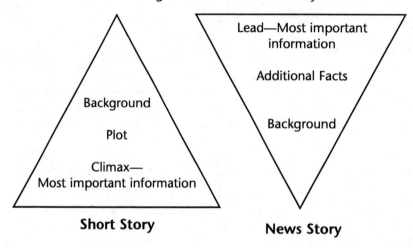

Reproduce Activity Sheet #7. Have newspapers available.

Newspapers
Distribute. Have students read the lead for one important news story on the front page.

Model
(a) Write WHO, WHAT, WHEN, WHERE, WHY, HOW on the board. Have students volunteer the facts from the lead that fit these factual categories.

(b) Analyze with the students the succinct language of the lead. Discuss the very first words of the lead. (Note: news stories rarely start with WHEN.)

(c) Have students read the rest of the news story. Discuss quotes within the news story.

(d) Draw the Inverted Pyramid on the board. Explain that news stories are organized with the most important information first so the reader pressed for time need only read a few paragraphs to learn the basic facts of the story. Also, editors who run out of space for the entire article know that they can cut off the bottom part of the story without losing essential information.

Objective
Tell students today they will write a news story based on the central conflict in the novel or other literary work they are reading. They are the **reporters**.

Activity Sheet
Distribute. *Assign Step 1.* Allow time to complete, then discuss. *Note:* the 5 Ws and the H usually appear in the first or second paragraphs. Not all news stories carry every one of the 5 Ws and H in the lead paragraphs. Feature stories are often written in a different structure and these elements may not be as obvious.

Assign Step 2. Allow time to complete then discuss.

Assign remaining steps. Circulate around the room to assist students with lead-writing and selection of remaining facts. Reminder: be accurate. Stick to the facts and quotations found in the novel!
Select the best news stories to save for class newspaper project.

Essay
Have students write an editorial (essay) giving the editor's opinion of the conflict in the news story. Explain that editorials derive from news. The news stories give the facts. The editorials give the paper's opinions.

Writing...a News Story about Conflict

Title of Novel: _____

1. Summarize the novel's central conflict in one sentence: _____

   _____

2. Now, list the important facts about the conflict:

   a) *Who* is in conflict? _____

   b) *What* happened? _____

   c) *When?* _____

   d) *Where?* _____

   e) *Why?* _____

3. On scratch paper, begin to write your news story. The first paragraph (the lead) contains all of the above facts. The first words in the paragraph should be the most important. The lead should be less than 20 words.

4. Revise your lead and write it below.

   _____

   _____

   _____

   _____

   _____

   _____

   _____

   _____

5. On the back of this paper, make a list of additional background facts to include in your news story. Create quotations from dialogue in the book.

6. Now, write the rest of your news story, using short sentences. Each paragraph should be less than 20 words.

7. Revise. Type up your news story with the lead first.

Writing...Photo Captions Illustrating Conflict in a Novel

Outcome
Students will be able to identify conflict in a novel and write about it succinctly and accurately.

Skills Used
Analysis, synthesis, selecting concise vocabulary.

Preparation
Choose a selection clearly describing a conflict between characters, or between a character and nature, in a novel your students are reading. Scan today's local newspaper for pictures of conflicts. Select one to use as a model. Reproduce Activity Sheet #8. Have newspapers available.

Ask
What is a conflict? Are conflicts always between people? Are conflicts always violent?

Objective
Tell students today they will learn how to write a caption for a picture about a conflict in the novel they are reading.

Model
Distribute newspapers. Discuss the types of conflict shown in the photos: a conflict between people (crime, sports, etc.), or a conflict pitting people against nature, or a conflict within an individual character. Focus on your model photo. Read the caption aloud. Write answers to the following questions on the board:

Ask
WHO or WHAT is the conflict? WHERE is the conflict? WHY is there a conflict? TYPE of conflict? What is the central conflict in (the novel the students are reading now)? Have students draw a picture of the central conflict. Or if possible, take instant photographs of a staged version of the conflict. Have the class as a whole write a caption for the picture. First, write WHO, WHAT, WHERE on the board and fill in the words volunteered. Then count the words. Revise on the board so the caption is accurate, interesting, and less than 30 words. Introduce the Thesaurus as a resource. Identify the type of conflict.

Activity Sheet
Distribute. Form collaborative groups of 3–4 students. Assign a specific chapter to each group. Students decide what the conflict is in the assigned chapter. They may either draw the conflict or stage the conflict and use a camera to make the picture. (If photographing, set time for each group to stage and photograph. Call class to order to watch the production.) *Note:* Have each group select a leader. The leader needs to engage each student in her or his group.

Followup Discussion
When groups have completed their activity, have leader report to full class: give chapter, summarize the conflict, show picture, read caption. Class checks for accuracy (understanding the conflict, clear depiction, succinct writing.) Save for class newspaper project.

Essay Topic
Write an essay comparing the conflict in the novel with conflicts reported in the newspaper. Why are the conflicts similar or different?

23

Writing...Photo Captions Illustrating Conflict in a Novel

Title of Novel: _____

Chapter: _____

1. List below the major conflict in the chapter:

   Conflict is between: _____

   Conflict is about: _____

   _____

   _____

   _____

   Type of conflict: _____

   _____

2. Create a picture of this conflict on another sheet of paper.

3. (a) On scratch paper, write a first-draft of a caption that tells all the important information about the conflict shown in your picture.
   (b) Revise. Use very descriptive words. Limit: 30 words.
   (c) When your caption is accurate and fits the space, write it below:

   _____
   _____
   _____
   _____
   _____
   _____
   _____
   _____
   _____
   _____

Writing...a News Story about a Character's Crime

Outcome
Students will write a concise, accurate report of a character's crime, in news story format.

Skills Used
Research, analysis, powerful vocabulary.

Preparation
Find a news story about a crime in today's newspaper. Review the 5 Ws and H and Inverted Pyramid news story style in Teacher Plan for Lesson #7.
Review and reproduce Activity Sheet #9.
Have newspapers available.

Ask
When someone is accused of a crime, is he or she guilty? *(No. Guilt is determined in a court of law by a jury.)*

Objective
Tell students today they will write a news story about a crime committed by a character in a novel.

Newspapers
Distribute. Ask students to read the crime story you've selected.

Model
Write **Who, What, When, Where, Why, How** on the board. Have students fill in the information from the news story. Discuss how much information there is in the lead (first paragraph).
Have students read the balance of the story. Discuss the other facts. Review writing of a news story from Lesson #7.

Activity Sheet
Distribute. *Assign Step 1.* If more than one crime occurs in the story, assign different characters to different students. Discuss the 5 Ws and H for the lead. Assign *Steps 2 and 3.* Circulate and help students with organizing the story's facts into the Inverted Pyramid. Save the best stories for class newspaper project.

Writing...a News Story about a Character's Crime

Title of Novel: _____

1. ***Who*** committed the crime (which character in book)? _____

   What kind of crime? _____

   When? _____

   Where? _____

   Why? _____

   How? _____

2. Write a lead paragraph for a news story about this crime. Start with the most important fact. Maximum: 20 words. Use short, snappy sentences. Draft on scratch paper, then revise. Print final version below.

   _____

   _____

   _____

   _____

   _____

   _____

   _____

   _____

   _____

3. List the other facts and background to help tell the story of the crime on scratch paper.

   Number the facts in order of importance.

   Write the rest of your crime story in the Inverted Pyramid style: most important facts first, then lesser important facts in succeeding paragraphs. Use quotations taken from the dialogue in the story.

   Be accurate. And remember, use the terms "the accused" (not "the killer") and "the alleged" crime—because a suspect is innocent until proven guilty in a court of law. Do not convict the alleged killer in print!

Writing...a Comic Strip about a Novel

Outcome
Students will graphically demonstrate knowledge of plot.

Skills Used
Sequencing, analyzing.

Preparation
Scan the comics. Identify those that have a beginning, middle, and end. Identify those that are ongoing. Reproduce Activity Sheet #10. Have newspapers available. Have scratch paper available for illustrating comics.

Newspapers
Distribute. Have students read the comics.

Ask
Which comic strip tells a story? Is it a complete story or part of an ongoing story? Which comics have dialogue in "balloons"? What is the purpose of the dialogue?

Objective
Tell students today they will create a comic strip from the plot of the novel (or other literary work) they are reading.

Management
Divide students into collaborative groups of 4–5 each. If you know certain students have artistic talent, assign to different groups. Tell groups to choose a leader, illustrators, and writers. Everyone in each group will be responsible for listing the plot points on the Activity Sheet.

Activity Sheet
Distribute. Review with students. If there are more than eight major plot points in the story, advise students to use the back of the Activity Sheet. *Assign Step A.* Circulate and check for understanding. Also check on role assignments within groups. When groups have listed plot points, *assign Step B.*

Followup
Students should sign their comics. Post in the room, and save for class newspaper project.

Writing...a Comic Strip about a Novel

Title of Novel: _____

A. Make a list of the most important turning points in this novel and the characters involved. Your list should start at the beginning and go step-by-step to the end. Be sure to describe what happened and which characters were involved.

First, _____
_____
_____

Second, _____
_____
_____

Next, _____
_____

And then, _____
_____

After that, _____
_____

The plot thickens when _____
_____
_____
_____

A major turning point was _____
_____
_____
_____

Finally, _____
_____
_____
_____
_____

B. For each step in the plot, use a separate sheet of paper for each frame of the comic strip. Draw the situation. Write in the dialogue in "balloons" above your comic strip characters. Be accurate to the story you are reading.

Writing...a Movie Ad for a Novel

Outcome
Students will demonstrate their understanding of a novel by writing a movie advertisement.

Skills Used
Analysis, vocabulary-building.

Preparation
Scan the movie ads. Note descriptive language, quotations from critics. Also read the reviews and news reports about current films. (*Note:* Friday newspaper will have larger ads, and more reviews.)

Reproduce Activity Sheet #11. Have newspapers, thesauri, dictionaries, and scratch paper available.

Newspapers
Distribute. Tell students to read the movie ads.

Ask
How do you choose to see a particular movie? What words in which ads help you make that decision? What do you think about the quotations by the critics? After you go to a movie, what do you tell your friends? Do they agree with you? Why or why not?

Objective
Tell students today they will write a movie ad for the novel (or other literary work) they are reading.

Activity Sheet
Distribute. *Assign Step A.* Then discuss. *Assign Step B.* Circulate and assist students with vocabulary. Remind students to be accurate in describing their characters. They will find help by searching the novel for descriptions and statements by other characters. *Assign Step C.* Have students avoid very general terms like "it's great!" *Assign Step D.* Circulate, encourage students to revise, try again. Transfer finished ads to back of Activity Sheet. Share and save.

Extension Activity
Have students read movie reviews and write a review of a movie made from a novel.

Writing...a Movie Ad for a Novel

Title of Novel: _____

A. Summarize the conflict: _____

_____

_____

_____

_____

_____

B. List the main characters and some words describing them:

Main Characters	**Two Adjectives about Each**
1. _____	_____
	_____
2. _____	_____
	_____
3. _____	_____
	_____

C. Pretend you are a critic. Give your opinion of this novel as a movie in five words or less. Your words should express your feelings: _____

_____

_____

_____

_____

D. On scratch paper, draw a box. Fit in the best words about the plot and the characters—so people will want to come and see this movie. Use large-size letters and smaller letters, too. However, the words themselves are the most important. Be accurate to the story.

When you like the way your ad looks and reads, copy it on the back of this sheet.

Writing...Real Estate Ads about Fictional Properties

Outcome
Students will demonstrate their understanding of the setting of a novel by writing a real estate ad for the characters.

Skills Used
Research, analysis, compare and contrast.

Preparation
Select a paragraph rich in description of the setting for the novel—the dwelling where the characters live. Scan the real estate for-sale and for-rent ads in the Classified section of your local newspaper. Compare advertised dwellings to the dwelling of the characters, for use as a model lesson. Review and reproduce Activity Sheet #12. Have newspapers available.

Motivation
Have students write a description of their own homes, the place where they live. Have them think about how their home fits all the people who live there. This should be a silent exercise.

Ask
How do people choose places to live? Do they always have a choice?

Objective
Tell students today they will learn to write a real estate ad for the place where the characters in a novel live.

Newspapers
Distribute. Have students read through the for-sale and for-rent ads in the Classified section. Select one as a model and read aloud.

Ask
What kind of people would buy/rent this dwelling? Could they have pets? What kind? Would this be a good place for children? What about the size? What kind of income would it take to buy or rent this?

Activity Sheet
Form pairs of students. Distribute. Complete Title and Residence lines. Discuss the type of residence. This could be a castle, a mud hut, a campsite, an apartment, a two-story house—wherever the characters have their primary residence. Then *assign Step A.* Guide students to use descriptive words. Discuss. Write on board. *Assign Step B.* Circulate and assist students in identifying the special needs of the characters in the novel. Some characters may need a secret exit, or servants' quarters, or a room for grandmother on the main floor. Stress accuracy—the needs must be based on the story. Discuss how much money the characters have and how this affects their choice of dwelling in the story. *Assign Steps C and D.* Remind students to draft their ads on scratch paper, then revise, and write a final version, up to 30 words, on the Activity Sheet.

Followup
Share and discuss the ads. Save the best ads for the class newspaper project.

Essay Topic
Extension or extra-credit activity: students write an essay—"Why I would or would not like to live where the characters live."

Background on Newspaper Careers in Advertising
See Teacher Plan #1.

Writing...Real Estate Ads about Fictional Properties

Title of Novel: _____

Type of Residence: _____

A. Find the words that describe this residence. (Note the pages they appear on.)

_____
_____
_____
_____
_____
_____

B. Pretend that the characters in the novel are looking for a place to live. You will write an ad about this residence (setting) that will attract these characters. First, describe the characters:

How many in family? _____   How many children? _____
How many pets? _____   Type of pets? _____

Special needs of individual characters:

_____
_____
_____
_____
_____
_____

C. Decide if your characters would be looking for a place to buy or rent, based on the story. Start to write a For-Sale or For-Rent ad on scratch paper. Refer to the ads in the Classified section of newspaper for hints. Limit: 30 words.

D. Revise your ad until it fits into 30 words and is accurate for the story. Then write your finished ad here:

_____
_____
_____
_____
_____

Writing...a Clothing Ad for a Fictional Character

Outcome
Students will demonstrate their understanding of how the clothing worn by characters in a novel fits the setting and time period by creating a clothing ad for one of the characters.

Skills Used
Research, analysis, application of information.

Preparation
Select a minor character in the novel (or other literary work) your students are reading and find descriptive information about this character. Review clothing ads in today's local newspaper to see if any clothing could have been worn by the character. If not, be prepared to sketch the clothing, or select an artistic student to do so. Give this student the assignment several days ahead of this lesson.

Ask
How do you select the clothes you wear? (Discuss weather, comfort, stylishness, etc.)

Objective
Tell students today they will learn to write a clothing advertisement about one of the characters in the novel they are reading.

Newspapers
Distribute. Have students review the clothing ads and circle the clothes they would wear in their daily lives.

Ask
What words motivate you to buy these clothes? What pictures motivate you to buy these clothes?

Model
Write the name of the minor character on the board. Have students find words that describe the character's attire in the story. Discuss. Have students find ads with clothing this character could have worn in the story, or have an artistic student show illustrations prepared ahead of time.

Activity Sheet
Distribute. Form pairs or small groups. Assign different groups different characters to research. Circulate and assist students with the various steps in creating their ad.

Followup
Share ads. Save the best ads for the class newspaper project.

Essay
"Why I Like or Dislike the Clothing of This Character."

Background on Newspaper Careers
"The variety that comes with advertising jobs is appealing. One morning you'll be in the office, brainstorming with clients about ad copy and layout to launch a product. That afternoon you'll be out and about—visiting shops, calling on advertisers, and selling the services of your newspaper..."

"At large newspapers, the advertising and marketing departments include market research analysts, artists, writers, marketing and media planners, sales professionals, telemarketers, technology specialists, account representatives, color experts, and a host of other career options. At smaller newspapers, one person may have several responsibilities..."

(Newspaper: *What's in It for Me: Your Complete Guide to Newspaper Careers.* Published by the Newspaper Association of America Foundation Reston, VA revised 1992. Pages 2–3.)

© Novel Units, Inc.

35

Writing...a Clothing Ad for a Fictional Character

Title of Novel: _____

Character: _____

1. Find information in the novel you are reading that describe the clothing this character wears. Note the page number where you find the information for future reference.

   My character wears:

   _____
   _____
   _____
   _____
   _____
   _____
   _____
   _____

2. Pretend your character is going shopping and looks in the newspaper to find ads for this kind of clothing. Create an ad about clothes for this character. Be true to the story. Review the clothing ads in the newspaper to give you ideas for vocabulary.

3. Write a headline for the ad.

   _____
   _____

4. Do a rough sketch of the clothes on scratch paper.

5. Draw your final ad with words and illustrations.

Did your character change his/her "image" during the story? You may want to create an ad for each "image." Identify when the change takes place in the story in a footnote to your ad.

Writing...an Article about a Fictional Party

Outcome
Students will be able to synthesize facts into a new whole.

Skills Used
Research, analysis, synthesis, observation.

Preparation
Select two articles from your local newspaper: one about food and another reporting a social event, such as a party at some prominent person's home. Use as models. Select some paragraphs rich in detail about the characters' living habits—eating, socializing—in a novel or other literature your students are reading. Reproduce Activity Sheet #14. Have newspapers available. Decide if you will use pairs or small groups for Step B.

Ask
Have you ever given a party? How did you prepare? Where did you hold the party? How did you decide what kind of food to serve?

Newspapers
Distribute and have students read the two articles you have selected. Discuss with the objective of sharpening your students' observation of **setting** in the novel.

Ask
What kind of food goes with what kind of party? Who attended the party? Why? Where was the party held?

Objective
Tell students today they will plan a party for some of the characters in the novel they are reading. Then they will write an article reporting it.

Activity Sheet
Distribute. *Assign Step A* for reinforcement. Circulate. Discuss. *Assign Step B.* This can be a good activity for pairs or small groups as a party-planning committee. Circulate and check for understanding of the planning needed **based on facts in the story**. *Assign Step C.* Have all students write individually. Then they regroup, share writings, and select the best paragraphs to include in the final report. (Note: complicated news stories are sometimes written by a team of reporters. Each reporter is assigned to a different aspect of the story.)

Followup
Groups share articles. Save the best ones for the class newspaper project.

Essay Topic
As an extension activity, assign students to write an essay on the best or worst party they have ever attended. Another topic: "our special family holiday food and what it means to me."

Extension Activity
Have the party! Students make the food and role-play the characters.

Name: _____

Writing...an Article about a Fictional Party

Title of Novel: _____

A. (1) Look in the Food section of your local newspaper. Read the articles and notice how the recipes are set up.

   (2) Now, read about parties in the society or social pages of your local newspaper. Notice how the report talks about the food and who was there.

B. You are planning a party for the characters in this fictional story. Look through the book and find information about food and the layout of the place where they live. Note pages for future reference.

   Food:

   _____
   _____
   _____
   _____
   _____
   _____

   Setting Available for the Party:

   _____
   _____
   _____
   _____
   _____
   _____

   Characters Attending the Party:

   _____
   _____
   _____
   _____
   _____
   _____

C. Write an article about a pretend party you have given for the characters in this book. Include **who, what, when, where, why**. Talk about the food and the setting. Examples: Who spoke to whom on the patio or in the cave? Who ate what in the kitchen or the attic?

   Remember, *all your facts must be taken from the book*. But use your imagination. Pretend you are there at the party! What do you see? Write it down!

Writing...a Garage Sale Ad for Characters in a Novel

Outcome
Students will write concisely and select powerful words.

Skills Used
Editing, revising, scanning, character analysis.

Preparation
Choose a selection rich in detail about the setting from the work your students are reading. Locate the garage sale ads in the Classified section of your local newspaper. A Friday paper is best. Reproduce Activity Sheet #15. Have newspapers available.

Ask
Have you ever gone to a garage sale? What have you bought or sold at garage sales? What do the items for sale tell you about the people selling them?

Objective
Tell students today they will learn how to write a garage sale ad for a character in a novel.

Model
In a few paragraphs, have students find items belonging to one of the characters who will be having a garage sale. List on the board. Describe concisely. Example: "one slightly-used caldron" owned by the witches in *Macbeth*.

Activity Sheet
Distribute. Form pairs. *Assign Step 1.* (10 minutes)

Newspapers
Distribute. Find Classified section and locate garage sales. Have students read aloud.

Ask
Which garage sales would you go to? Why or why not? (Discuss words that "sell.") What must a garage sale ad include? Do Step 2. Which newspaper will your garage sale for the character be published in? (the newspaper for the town where the story takes place)

Activity Sheet
Explain Steps 3 and 4. Count the letters and spaces in the list on the board to show students how words take up space. Circulate around the room and guide students in their first draft on scratch paper. After students write their first draft, have them count the letters and spaces and revise to fit the ad into three lines of 25 characters each. Print on spaces provided. Read finished ads aloud. Save for the newspaper project at end of this unit.

Independent Practice
Assign a similar exercise for homework. Students choose a character from another fictional work.

Writing...a Garage Sale Ad for Characters in a Novel

Title of Novel: _____

Name of Character in Novel: _____

Pretend you are this character. You are planning a garage sale and will sell your items.

1. Search through the novel and make a list below of unique and interesting things belonging to this character (or the character's family) that you will sell at the garage sale.

Items	*Page #*

2. Find the garage sale ads in the Classified section of the local newspaper. Underline words that get your attention, items you want to see at that garage sale.

3. Now, use a piece of scratch paper to practice writing your ad for your fictional character. Include the items you listed above. You have $15.00 to spend for your ad. That will buy three lines of 25 characters each line. Write, then count the characters. Revise until you fit the space allowed with the most interesting words.

4. Print your finished ad below:

_ _

_ _

_ _

(Each small line equals one letter in a word or a space between the words.)

A Newspaper about a Novel

Outcome
Students will demonstrate their complete understanding of a novel by creating a newspaper composed of material from the novel: news stories, opinion, columns, display ads, classified ads, feature stories, captions for photos.

Skills Used
Organization, management, analysis, ranking.

Newspapers
Assemble files of the material you have saved from the various lessons—the best examples of articles, ads, etc. It is wise to keep photocopies of these for yourself, as students could lose the material during the process of creating the newspaper. Have newspapers available for reference. Assign students to roles. Make chart:

- **Editor:** supervises Editorial/Opinion pages: the "voice" of the paper. Establishes policy for Managing Editor to implement. Decides on the "look" of the newspaper.

- **Managing Editor:** supervises the assembly of the paper. Decides what kind of news goes on each page, decides what stories go on front page.

- **News Editor:** dummies the page (layout), after the Editorial Conference ("budget meeting").

- **Copy Editor:** writes the headlines and edits the copy for all the stories that go into the newspaper. Often uses a computer to fit the stories into the space that the News Editor dummies. Okays each page after composition has pasted up all the parts. Has a staff to help.

- **City Editor:** assigns news reporters to specific stories. Edits stories (looking for "holes" in stories). Receives phone calls from the public suggesting potential news stories or factual errors, and critiquing stories already in the paper.

- **Reporters:** write specific stories as assigned. Can also be assigned to a "beat," such as Police Department or Schools or Courts.

- **Photo Editor:** responsible for all photos. Works with City Editor to decide which stories will need photos. Assigns photographers; can also take photos.

- **Photographers:** take photos as assigned (For class newspaper, stage from content of the novel.)

- **Artists:** illustrate stories, make charts to explain complicated stories, based on assignments from the City Editor. If small paper, also illustrate display ads.

- **Display Advertising Manager:** supervises display ad sales reps who get large, illustrated ads for the newspaper. Assigns accounts (such as department stores, grocery stores) to specific reps. Dummies ads on the pages before the news stories go on. (The remaining space on a page is called "the news hole.")

- **Display Advertising Sales Reps:** work with the advertising customer to create the display ads.

- **Classified Sales Manager:** supervises classified telephone sales reps. Dummies Classified pages.

- **Classified Sales Representatives:** take calls from people wanting to advertise garage sales, employment ads, cars and other items for sale, lost dogs, etc. Help customers write the ads.

- **Composing Manager:** supervises paste-up of all the pages, to create camera-ready pages.

- **Compositors:** operate the computer or other equipment to set the stories into type. Also create headlines and text material for ads.

- **Printer:** takes camera-ready pages and prints them.(If commercial printing not available, pages can be photocopied.)

Other possible positions, if your newspaper becomes a very large project:

- **Features Editor:** assigns non-news stories, usually "human interest" in-depth stories, or articles about social trends.

- **Sports Editor:** creates the sports page; assigns sports reporters to cover sporting events.

- **Business Editor:** creates the Business page; assigns business reporters to stories.

Objective
Tell students they will spend the next 4–5 class periods creating a newspaper from the novel they are reading. Assign roles. Discuss each student's role. Have them write down their responsibilities.

Ask
What shall we call this newspaper? (Decide on name appropriate to the novel.) What sections should the newspaper have? (Use local newspaper as model.) What size should the pages be? (Limit to 11" x 17" to save printing cost.)

Instruction
Explain the different jobs on the newspaper and announce role assignments. Hand key editors/managers the files you have been saving of student work in the various lessons. Tell students you have saved the best material from the lessons. The editors will use this material, but are free to create more. All students participate in a "budget meeting" to decide what stories go where. Managing Editor and News Editor make the list by page. Then students get into small groups with editor/manager and create the material necessary to fill the pages.

Followup
Distribute printed newspapers to all students, as well as teachers, administrators, and parents.

Notes

Notes